MW00990697

A Mouthful of

Murder

Frosted Love Cozy Mysteries

Book 4

New Revision

By

Summer Prescott

ISBN:9781720573005

Author's note: I'd love to hear your thoughts on my books, the storylines, and anything else that you'd like to comment on—reader feedback is very important to me. My contact information, along with some other helpful links, is listed below. If you'd like to be on my list of "folks to contact" with updates, release and sales notifications, etc.... just shoot me an email and let me know. Thanks for reading!

Also…

… if you're looking for more great reads, I am proud to announce that Summer Prescott Books publishes several popular series by Cozy author Patti Benning, as well as Carolyn Q. Hunter, Blair Merrin, Susie Gayle and more! Check out my book catalog http://summerprescottbooks.com/book-catalog/ for their delicious stories.

Contact Info for Summer Prescott:

Twitter: @summerprescott1

Blog and Book Catalog:

http://summerprescottbooks.com

Email:

summer.prescott.cozies@gmail.com

And…look up The Summer Prescott Fan Page and Summer Prescott Publishing Page on Facebook – let's be friends!

To sign up for our fun and exciting newsletter, which will give you opportunities to win prizes and swag, enter contests, and be the first to know about New Releases, click here:

https://forms.aweber.com/form/02/1682036 602.htm

TABLE OF CONTENTS

A Mouthful of Murder

Murder

Frosted Love Cozy Mysteries

Book 4

New Revision

CHAPTER ONE

Melissa Gladstone nodded appreciatively from her safe spot on the sidewalk. The sweet little cupcake shop, Missy's Frosted Love Cupcakes, which she had inherited upon the untimely death of her parents, was being rebuilt after a devastating fire, and seeing it rising from the ashes was a profound relief. Her second shop, Crème de la Cupcake, in the nearby town of Dellville, had opened shortly after the fire and was doing very well, with early morning customers lining up before the 6 a.m. opening time for coffee and a cupcake on the way to work.

The Dellville shop was thriving under the watchful eye of Ben Radigan, Missy's former assistant, who had been promoted to Manager of the new location. The new girl, Cheryl, whom she had hired after purchasing the new property, was working out well too. The vivacious young woman was pleasant and efficient, and had brought Ben, a sworn introvert, out of his shell quite a bit. Things had finally settled down for Missy, after a couple of hair-raising adventures, and she looked forward to a peaceful time of 'business as usual'.

Satisfied that the new construction was progressing well in LaChance, she guided her little burgundy car onto the two-lane highway that led to Dellville to check in with Ben and Cheryl.

"Hi, Ms. G.," Cheryl called out when Missy arrived at Crème de la Cupcake. "You just missed the tail end of the morning rush. Ben's in the back, loading up trays because we sold out of almost everything that we had up here," the bubbly brunette reported.

"Well, that's certainly good to hear," Missy smiled at her enthusiasm.

The bell jangled behind her, and she turned to see Clara Clements, the elderly owner of the ice cream shop across the street, shuffling in.

"I saw your car pull up and decided to come over and say hello," Clara announced with a cheery wave and broad smile.

"I'm glad you did. You look like you're in good spirits today," Missy observed, going over to give the tiny woman a hug.

"Oh yes dear, I really, really am," she nodded. "I have a buyer for the ice cream store. She's coming in from California this week, so I'll show her how everything works, then I'll be headed to Florida at the end of the month."

"Oh wow, congratulations, Clara!" Missy exclaimed. "That's great! If the new owner needs anything, you be sure to tell her to come over and see me."

"You know I will, dear. I think you two will hit it off immediately. She's about your age, single, no family that I know of."

"Hmm…that's interesting. What on earth brings her from California to Dellville, Louisiana if she doesn't even have family here?" Missy wondered.

Clara edged closer and lowered her voice. "Well, I couldn't figure that out either, but I'm thinking that there's something…or someone, that she was definitely ready to leave behind."

Missy nodded thoughtfully. "Well, if that's the case, I hope she makes a wonderful new start here. This town may be small, but it's friendly."

"Exactly my thought," the kindly woman agreed. "I'd better get back across the street – just wanted to share my good news."

"I'm glad you did, I'm so happy for you." They hugged again, and Clara shuffled back across the street.

Missy went to the back to check on Ben, and when she came back out to the front of the shop, satisfied that he had things well under control, she was delighted to see Detective Chas Beckett coming in the door.

"What great timing!" she beamed at the handsome detective, standing on tiptoe to give him a quick kiss on the cheek. "I was just about to go to lunch. Join me?"

"Yes, I'm starving," Chas agreed, holding the door open for her. "We can talk about Cora Nesbitt's mystery while we eat."

"Oh good, I'm looking forward to that, the poor dear."

Cora Nesbitt was a sweet, older woman from LaChance, who provided Missy with fresh peaches every summer. The cupcakes that she made from the peaches were legendary, and her regulars would line up early to get them before they sold out. A few weeks ago, shortly after the shop in LaChance had burned down, Cora had come to visit her at the new location, with a bizarre story to tell, looking for help with a dilemma that she was facing. Missy had immediately called Chas, and the two of them were trying to figure out how to help the frightened woman.

The couple sat down at a bistro table at a café down the street from Missy's shop, in the shade under a green and white striped awning, and ordered their lunch.

"So, what's going on with Cora?" Missy asked, anxious for news.

"The unfortunate reality is that she's definitely not imagining things. There really is someone coming into her house at night, there are items disappearing from her home, and there are absolutely no leads as to who might be doing such things. I advised her to take photos of all of her belongings so that she would know if anything went missing, and several items have, both inside and outside." Chas shook his head, frustrated. "I haven't come up with a single lead after talking with neighbors and family members."

"You don't suppose she's in danger, do you?" Missy frowned.

"At this point, there doesn't seem to be any indication of a threat to her personally, but any time there is an intruder in a residence, the potential for danger exists," he said grimly.

"I wish she had someone who could stay with her."

"Well, I have patrol cars doing surveillance several times a night. If the intruder keeps returning, we'll get them eventually," Chas assured her.

They dug into their lunches with gusto, talking about everything and nothing, simply enjoying each other's company, until Chas pushed back his plate. "As much as I'd love to spend the afternoon in your most pleasant company, duty calls," he grinned at her fondly. Fortunately, the distance between LaChance and Dellville was short enough that he could get away for a quick lunch from time to time.

"I understand. I need to get back to the shop anyway," Missy replied, already thinking about the tasks that awaited her.

The busy detective dropped Missy off at Crème de la Cupcake with a kiss on the cheek and a dinner invitation for later in the week. "Stay out of trouble," he teased.

"Always!" Missy winked.

**

Missy knew before she went into the shop this morning that it would be a busy day. Ben had come up with the idea of posting the Cupcake Flavor of the Day, for each day of the week, on a signboard in the front of the shop every Monday. Some varieties were more popular than others, and today's flavor, Mochaccino with Caramel Fluff, seemed to be a particular favorite. Just as she had anticipated, patrons were lined up in front of the store before Ben unlocked the front door, so Missy mingled and chatted with them while they waited. Once inside, time seemed to move in fast forward as one customer after another came in, made their selection, paid and left. A few sat at tables to enjoy their early morning treat, but most just passed thru on their way to work. When the last few in line had been served, it was nearly lunch time. Cheryl and Ben had just finished restocking the glass cases up front when the bell above the door jangled again. Missy looked up to see Clara Clements coming in with a woman who could only be the new owner of the ice cream store that she had mentioned.

"You've had quite the rush over here this morning," Clara observed.

"Yes, it was a little overwhelming, but the time just flew by," Missy agreed. "It's a good problem to have," she grinned.

"Absolutely," Clara agreed. "I waited to come over until things calmed down, but I'm just so excited to introduce you to the gal who is buying my store," she beamed, patting the arm of the woman who had come in with her. "Echo Willis, meet Melissa Gladstone. Missy, Echo," Clara introduced them. The newcomer had an abundance of coppery-red hair, and wore a gauzy taupe-colored camisole with a faded gingham skirt and brown leather sandals, looking very 'California'.

Missy held out her hand, "Hi, I'm Missy. It's great to meet you. Congratulations and welcome to the neighborhood."

"Nice to meet you too, thanks," the woman smiled, and Missy noticed that she had the most beautiful jade-green eyes.

"Let me get you two a cupcake and some coffee then we can sit down and chat for a bit," she offered, extending the hospitality for which her home state was known.

"Oh, no, thank you," Echo demurred quickly. "We have to get back across the street, the attorneys will be there with paperwork soon, we just wanted to come say hello," she explained. "I'll definitely come back by later this week though, so we can get to know each other better."

"That sounds great," Missy agreed, wondering what had suddenly made the new gal seem so nervous. Chalking it up to her being in an entirely new world with a whole new set of responsibilities, she dismissed her concerns and saw Clara and Echo to the door, wishing them well.

CHAPTER TWO

Missy had been working for a while on a new recipe for fluffy lemon cupcakes with a cream cheese frosting and a decorative drizzle of raspberry. Since Ben and Cheryl were doing a fantastic job of running the shop, she decided to head back to the kitchen to whip up a batch and see how they turned out. While the cupcakes were baking, she prepared the cream cheese frosting, which turned out beautifully light and fluffy. When the light-yellow cakes were cooling on the rack, she pureed luscious, ripe raspberries, combining them with raw sugar and her secret blend of flavors. After frosting and drizzling one of the moist, decadent lemon cupcakes, she took a huge bite, delighted to find that they had turned out even better than she had expected.

Frosting the rest of the batch, Missy decided to take two of her delightful creations up front for Ben and Cheryl to try. The combination of cream cheese, lemon and raspberry flavors was one of her favorites so far, but she wanted to get some unbiased opinions.

"Hey, you two," she called out, carrying a tray with the cupcakes to the front with her. "You have to try these and let me know what you think. They're my new lemon cupcakes with cream cheese frosting and raspberry," she finished, coming up to the counter and noticing that a rather scruffy looking customer was staring at her as she put down the tray. "Oh, hello, I didn't know that there was anyone in the shop. How are you today?" she greeted the man.

"Pretty good," the shaggy haired, bearded guy in a rainbow t-shirt, faded jeans and leather sandals said. "Those cupcakes sound good, do you have any more of that kind?" he peered over the counter curiously.

"Oh, sure," Missy said, caught off guard. "You can have one of these, and I'll get another one from the back."

"Thanks," he accepted the cupcake and took a large bite, making a face as he chewed.

"Oh dear, don't you like it?" she asked, worried.

"I'm not much of one for sweets," the man shrugged, swallowing hard.

Cheryl and Ben exchanged a shocked look. Missy thought that his response was a bit strange. Why on earth would he come into a cupcake shop if he didn't like sweets?

"Well, then, I won't charge you for the cupcake, since you didn't care for it," she offered.

This poor guy looked as though he was in need of a good meal, and perhaps couldn't afford one, so Missy couldn't, in good conscience, charge him for a cupcake that he didn't even like.

"That's cool," he nodded. "My mom would really be into this though…can I have one for her?"

Thinking that this was the oddest person that she'd met in a while, Missy told him that of course he could, and handed him a white paper bag with his mom's treat inside. Thanking her again, he pulled a piece of lime-green paper out of his pocket that he had torn from an advertisement on her bulletin board. Cora Nesbitt was looking for peach pickers and had put up the flyer with tear-away tabs that had her phone number on it.

"Hey, can I borrow your phone to call this lady? I'm looking for work," he explained.

"Certainly," Missy agreed, thinking that this strange stranger was really beginning to wear out his welcome.

She directed him to where Cheryl stood behind the counter and asked the hesitant young lady to hand him the phone. He got directions from Cora and headed over to pick peaches. Missy shook her head in disbelief when he popped the rest of his cupcake in his mouth as soon as he reached the sidewalk. Cheryl and Ben eagerly sampled the cupcakes after he left, and both gave her new creations a profound 'thumbs up'. She told the two of them to go ahead and leave for the day, since it was nearly closing time, then made a large batch of the luscious cupcakes for the next day. When she finally wrapped things up, Missy headed home to have a relaxing romp in the park with Toffee, her devoted Golden Retriever.

The enthusiastic animal greeted her owner with lots of happy doggy kisses, and soon the two of them were out the door, both eager for some fresh air and exercise. Missy had intentionally left her cell phone in the house while the two of them enjoyed their time in the park. When they had their outings, she didn't want to be distracted. Being able to focus on the joy and beauty of her best furry friend was one of her pleasures in life, and Missy gave it her full attention.

When the two of them settled in back at home, tired but happy, Toffee slurping fresh water from her bowl, and Missy sitting down for a cup of tea, she saw that she had several missed calls from Chas, along with a text message that said only, 'call me immediately when you receive this.' Puzzled, she hit the number one and 'send' on her phone to call the detective on his cell.

"Missy, where have you been?" Beckett said in a low voice when she answered the phone.

"Toffee and I went to the park to play fetch, why?" she asked, somewhat alarmed at his manner.

"Are you at home?" he ignored her question.

"Yes, of course. Chas, what is going on? Why are you acting so strangely?" she demanded, worried.

"Stay put, we'll talk when I get there."

He hung up without even waiting for a response. Missy was baffled. Chas was typically a man of few words, but his manners were always impeccable. She couldn't begin to imagine what might have happened that would cause him to be so short with her. Figuring that she'd find out soon enough, she hurriedly showered and changed into comfortable clothes, wrestling her curly golden locks into a casual ponytail. When Chas rang the doorbell a few minutes after she finished dressing, she opened the door with a smile, but his grim expression gave her pause. She invited him in, and they sat down in the living room.

"Chas, for heaven's sake, what is wrong?" she asked, frowning.

"The entire department is looking for you and has been alerted to bring you in for questioning when they find you. I know the routes that the guys have been taking, and you probably only have about twenty minutes before they show up. They've been cruising by your house at regular intervals. I've been told to stay away from you, due to an obvious conflict of interest, but I had to come over here to talk to you. I called your shop and there was no answer. Where were you this evening? Can you account for your time?" he asked, urgently.

"I left the shop around 6:00, came home, changed into athletic wear and took Toffee to the park. I got in just before I called you, why? What is going on,

Chas? Why do the police want to bring me in for questioning?" Missy was beginning to get scared.

"They need to speak with you as a possible witness, or person of interest in a homicide case."

"What?" she interrupted. "That's impossible! Wait, who died?" she asked, dreading the answer.

"Mrs. Nesbitt," Beckett answered softly. "I'm sorry."

Missy's hands flew to her mouth in shock and horror. "Oh no," she exclaimed, shaking her head, tears pooling in her eyes. "Not Cora. She was the sweetest…" she dissolved into tears.

"I knew that the two of you were friends, so it made no sense to me that you would be a suspect, but apparently there is some evidence that may implicate you." Chas grimaced.

"Evidence? What evidence? There can't be evidence of a crime that I didn't commit! Oh, this is horrible, Chas," she swiped her fingers under her eyes. "What happened to her, I mean…how did she…?" Missy couldn't finish the question.

Chas sighed, running a hand through his thick black hair in frustration. "I can't discuss the case with you, Missy, it wouldn't be good for either one of us. I'm going to go now, so no one can say that anything inappropriate has occurred, and there will probably be a squad car stopping by shortly. Just do what you always do, tell the truth and you'll be just fine." Chas stood to go, gathering the distraught woman into his arms for a gentle hug, then heading for the door.

CHAPTER THREE

Missy was frustrated as she sat through what felt like an interrogation with Detective, Gilbert Johnson, who occasionally assisted Chas in his investigations.

"Detective Johnson, I have told you three times now – I left the Crème de la Cupcake in Dellville around 6:00. From there, I came home, changed into athletic wear and took my dog, Toffee, to the park to play fetch. We got home from the park at about 6:45, and your officers arrived at my home around 7:15. What more is there to say?" she demanded, tired, hungry and impatient.

"Why do you think that there was a bushel basket full of peaches near Mrs. Nesbitt's back door that had a paper, with your name written on it, tucked into the basket?" the detective asked mildly, ignoring her protest.

"I have no idea, but offhand, I'd guess that she had planned to bring me a bushel of peaches so that I could make my peach cupcakes, like I do EVERY YEAR!" Missy shot back, appalled at the detective's insinuations. Cora Nesbitt was a sweet woman who was dear to her heart, and for the police to even suggest that she was involved in the precious lady's murder was offensive to the extreme.

"Did you see Mrs. Nesbitt today?" he asked, seemingly unfazed by her outburst.

"No, I did not."

"Did anyone in your shop see Mrs. Nesbitt today?" Johnson persisted.

"I doubt it. Cora always makes sure that she comes in whenever I'm there, so that we can chat and catch up."

"Would either of your staff members have mentioned it if Mrs. Nesbitt had come in during your absence?"

"Probably, because she would have asked them to give me her best," Missy said sadly, remembering the kind soul.

"So neither you, nor your staff saw Cora Nesbitt today, is that correct?"

"Right. Why?" Missy wondered where Gilbert Johnson was going with his line of questioning.

"Can you explain to me then, how it came to be that one of your cupcakes was on her table, sitting next to a cup of tea, when she died?"

"No, I can't explain it, unless someone else gave her one of my cupcakes." Missy gasped in horror as she had a sudden realization. "Detective, what kind of cupcake was it?" she demanded, a white-hot fury rising within her.

"What difference does it make?" Johnson narrowed his eyes, suspicious.

"If it was a lemon cupcake with cream cheese frosting and a drizzle of raspberry on top, I know who the killer might be," she gritted her teeth, remembering.

"For the sake of argument, who do you think the killer would be if it was a cupcake like you've just described?" he asked, avoiding answering directly.

"I don't know his name, but there was a strange man who came into my shop today. Ben, Cheryl and I were testing out a batch of lemon cream cheese cupcakes, and he asked if he could have one. I gave him one and he said he didn't like it, so I gave it to him for free, and then he finished it when he walked outside."

The detective regarded her with obvious skepticism. "Changing one's mind isn't a crime, Ms. Gladstone, and that doesn't even begin to explain why the cupcake was sitting on Cora's table."

"But it does," Missy insisted. "The man asked for another cupcake to take to his mother, so I gave him one, and before he left, he asked me if he could use the phone in the shop. He had to call for directions to Cora's place, because he said he needed work and she was advertising for peach pickers," Missy explained.

"So this 'strange man' knew Mrs. Nesbitt?" the detective raised an eyebrow.

"No, he pulled her phone number off of a flyer that she had put up on my bulletin board," she admitted sadly, now feeling partially to blame.

"Did the man give you his name?" Johnson resumed his rapid-fire questioning.

"No."

"Do you know if he's from around here?"

"He didn't sound like it. No drawl at all," Missy shook her head.

"Why didn't you just give him directions to Cora Nesbitt's home? You know where she lives, correct?"

"Well, yes, I've been to her house," Missy nodded.

"Then why didn't you just tell the man how to get there?" Johnson's eyes narrowed.

"I didn't even think of that," Missy murmured. "He was just so odd, that all I could think of was getting him out of my store."

"Yet you let him use your phone," the detective observed, eyes narrowed.

"It seemed like the polite thing to do," color rose in Missy's cheeks as she realized how guilty she must sound.

"I'm going to need you to come with me," Detective Johnson stated flatly.

"Where are we going?" she asked, alarmed.

"Dellville."

Missy sat behind Gilbert Johnson in his unmarked car for the ride to her shop, and noted that they were being followed by a patrol car, which had pulled in behind them when they left the police station. She unlocked the front door of Crème de la Cupcake, and the detective allowed her to enter, but instructed her not to touch anything. A technician dusted her phone for fingerprints, collected the flyer from the bulletin board, and discovered a cupcake wrapper that had been tossed away on the front sidewalk. After the police finished their investigation, and had taken notes on the description of the stranger, Missy locked up and rode back to the station with Detective Johnson.

"I appreciate your cooperation today, Ms. Gladstone, but I'll remind you that you're still a person of interest in this case, so you may not leave town without telling us first," Johnson directed, his tone coolly professional. Missy definitely preferred it to his former hostility.

"I have to leave town to run my business, Detective," Missy reminded him.

"That's fine, but no further than Dellville without prior permission," he responded curtly.

"I understand."

CHAPTER FOUR

Not only was Missy dismayed to find herself under scrutiny for the murder of someone whom she'd considered to be a friend, but she also had to endure that awful speculation without the support and help of Detective Chas Beckett. She knew that if she could just talk to him about the case, they'd be able to piece together what had happened to poor Mrs. Nesbitt.

Cora's insufferable nephew, Ian, was her only living relative, a ne'er do well who lived off of the remains of an inheritance garnered when his parents were tragically drowned off the coast of Maine in a boating accident. He had apparently taken up residence in his aunt's sprawling Victorian the moment her body had been removed from the premises.

41

Police had investigated Cora's home, and from the brief report that Chas had been able to share when he came in under the guise of buying cupcakes for the guys on patrol, some evidence had been gathered at the scene of the crime that could shed some light on the case. Missy asked him how Cora had died, but he couldn't divulge the information to her while she was still under investigation.

To help take her mind off of things, Missy extended her hours at work, baking and freezing hundreds of cupcakes to keep the cases well stocked. She took long strolls with Toffee, and attempted to lose herself in a good novel or two, but found that she couldn't concentrate on anything for very long. She was alone in the commercial kitchen in her Dellville shop one evening when she heard a knock at the back door. Wiping her hands on her apron, she opened it to find Echo Willis, the new owner of the ice cream shop across the street. Clara Clements, the former owner, of whom Missy had grown quite fond, had moved to Florida the past week, leaving Echo to run the business on her own.

"Hi Echo, how nice to see you again," Missy said with a smile that was a bit forced. She really wasn't in the mood for company, but her southern upbringing absolutely wouldn't allow her to turn away a guest. "Won't you come in?"

"Thanks, I'd like that," she replied. "I know it's after hours, but I saw lights on over here and thought I'd come make sure that everything was okay."

"Well, aren't you sweet? Everything is fine. I just find myself with way too much time on my hands these days, so I stay later and later preparing for business a week in advance," Missy shrugged, unaware of how sad she sounded.

"Well, if you don't mind having company, I have some spare time on my hands too," Echo admitted.

"Actually, it would be great to have someone to talk to, I'm glad you came over," Missy smiled, realizing that talking to someone new would be a great distraction from her thoughts. "I just pulled a batch of Crème Brulee cupcakes out of the oven if you'd like one," she offered.

"Oh, about that," Echo began, seeming embarrassed. "I'm vegan, and I have been my entire life, so it'd probably make me really sick if I tried one. That's why I didn't have a cupcake when I came over here the first time with Clara. I just didn't want to offend you."

"Oh my goodness, why didn't you say so?" Missy asked. "I have at least one or two vegan choices every day. In fact, when I went to a national cupcake competition in Vegas, my prize cupcake entry was a Vegan Coco Loco."

Echo giggled at the name. "That's awesome," she grinned.

"I love your outfit," Missy remarked, taking in the brick-red harem pants, ivory halter and wooden bangles that were scented lightly with patchouli.

"Thanks, it's really comfortable. I'm kind of a low-maintenance gal," Echo chuckled.

"That makes life easier," Missy nodded.

The two women chatted and laughed like old friends for a couple of hours while Missy baked to her heart's content, even whipping up a couple batches of vegan strawberry-banana cupcakes so that her new friend could take some home for the next day's breakfast. The silence seemed to close in on Missy, once Echo left, and after cleaning up the kitchen, she scoured the floors and polished every available surface. Having worked herself into exhaustion, Missy finally turned out the lights and locked the back door, headed for home.

A glimmer of light outside caught her eye as she did one final check of the seating area before she left, and she went to the window to determine the source of it. In the darkness, the entire town of Dellville seemingly slept, with not even a car passing by on the main street, but there was a vehicle turning into the drive behind the ice cream shop. She faintly saw shadowy figures entering and leaving the little shop, and wondered what on earth could be happening over there after nine o'clock at night, when the rest of the town was tucked in tight. She watched for a bit but couldn't really make out what was happening in the darkness, so she headed for her car and drove home, thinking of her new friend and hoping that she was okay.

CHAPTER FIVE

Missy had just returned from a morning jog with Toffee, sweat beading on her brow as she fed the dog and refilled her water bowl, when she heard her doorbell ring. Putting down the bowl of fresh, clean water for Toffee, she went to see who had stopped by. She hadn't been expecting company, and was more than a bit surprised when she opened the door and saw Ian Nesbitt, Cora Nesbitt's nephew on her front porch.

"Hello, Ian," Missy said coolly, never having been a fan of the hedonistic young man who used his aunt shamelessly whenever he needed money, a place to stay, or a reference for something.

"Mornin' Miss Gladstone," his voice oozed liquid Southern velvety charm. "How are you this fine day?"

"Hot, sweaty and in need of a shower," she responded. "What can I do for you?"

Not accustomed to being brushed off by women of any age, Ian was nonplussed.

"Actually, I came by to see if you'll still be wanting Aunt Cora's peaches for your business…or pleasure," his eyes slowly trailed up and down Missy's curvaceous figure, making her want to splash a glass of cold water in his face.

"Of course I'll still want the peaches," her tone was entirely professional. "Just have them delivered as usual," she moved to shut the door, but he stopped it with the toe of his expensive alligator shoe.

"I'm sorry, I'm not familiar with Auntie Cora's process, so it'll be much easier if you come by and get the peaches yourself," he leered.

"I really don't think that's a good idea, Ian, considering that the police are investigating me in connection with her death," Missy bit out, going for shock value.

"That's utter nonsense," he drawled, clearly not impressed. "There's no way in the world that a sweet little thing like you could be involved in that nasty business."

"Well, at any rate, I think it's best that I don't visit her house any time soon," Missy insisted, resolving not to lose her temper.

"Alright, darlin', I'll get you set up with some deliveries, and I'll be happy to come collect the payment personally," he raised his eyebrows suggestively.

"I'll mail it," Missy stated firmly, shutting the door.

She heard his obscene chuckle on the other side of the door and shuddered a bit. She had always had a bad feeling about that man, and now he didn't even have his maiden aunt around to keep him in line.

While she felt sorry for his loss, she seriously doubted that he even realized how much his aunt had cared for him.

**

"Hey, I hope I'm not interrupting," Echo Willis murmured, looking troubled when Missy opened the back door of the shop, having heard a soft knock as she was taking a batch of cupcakes out of the oven.

"Nope, once this batch cools down enough for me to get them frosted, I'll be done with my prep. What's on your mind? You look upset," Missy observed.

"Well, I really shouldn't be upset, I'm probably just being silly, but something kind of weirded me out yesterday and I wanted to talk to you about it, since you know so many people in this area," Echo folded her arms together as though she'd just had a slight chill.

"Sure, darlin', what's wrong?" Missy frowned.

"This guy came by, really late last night and he seemed...overly friendly, if you know what I mean. He said his name was Ian and that he wanted to welcome me to the area, but when we were talking, he said he lived in LaChance, which is the next town over," Echo explained. "Anyway, he was trying to sell me some peaches from his grandmother's farm or something, and..."

"Aunt's," Missy interrupted, shaking her head.

"Huh?"

"It's his aunt's farm, not his grandmother's. You were talking to Ian Nesbitt. His Aunt Cora owned an orchard in LaChance, and it belongs to him now," Missy informed her new friend. "He's nauseating, but harmless, as far as I know," she shrugged. "He came over here too, and I shooed him away."

"Oh good, I'm glad to hear you say that," Echo was relieved.

"Just show him that you're the one in control and that you're not interested, and you'll be fine," Missy advised.

"Goodness knows I don't have any problem doing that," Echo chuckled. "When you're all alone in this world, you have to be pretty tough to survive."

"Well, as long as I'm right across the street, you're never alone, right?" Missy smiled.

"Right," Echo nodded, giving her arm a squeeze. "Well, I don't want to keep you, I've got a million things to do and I'm sure you do too but thank you so much for the information. I'm relieved."

"Anytime, really. Just come on over here if you need anything."

"Thanks, I will," Echo headed out the door. "I'm loving this whole southern hospitality thing," she grinned.

"Oh honey, you ain't seen nothing yet," Missy laughed, waving to her new friend.

CHAPTER SIX

Missy shook her head as she saw the new sign going up on the ice cream shop across the street. Dellville was a pretty open-minded and friendly town that seemed to roll with whatever changes the outside world brought in, but she wasn't quite sure just how well a vegan ice cream shop would fare. Echo had brought over the new menu for the shop, which she was calling 'Sweet Love,' showing Missy the wide variety of selections that she had to offer, none of which contained any sort of animal products.

There were 'ice creams' made from soy, almond milk, rice milk and much more, in flavors that probably few people in Dellville had ever heard of. Personally, Missy was very much looking forward to trying the Red Chile Pepper Carob. Echo swore that a shop just like this had been a tremendous hit in

California, and Missy just hoped that she would be as successful here. The grand opening would be going on tomorrow, and since Echo's shop would be busiest after Missy's had already closed for the day, she was looking forward to going over and supporting her new friend.

Missy was going over a shopping list with Ben at the front counter, when she looked up and, across the street, she saw the scraggly-looking man who had left a lemon cream cheese cupcake at Cora Nesbitt's house on the day of her murder. By the time Missy came around the counter and ran out the front door, the man was halfway down the block. When she shouted to him, he glanced over his shoulder and took off, running. Her feet pounded the sidewalk, and she followed him as closely as she could, not knowing what she would do if she ever caught up to him. When he kept going, knowing that she was behind him, she began to wonder if he was intentionally leading her somewhere that might be hazardous to her well-being. He ducked into an alley that was a little too private and a little too dark for

Missy's taste, and she called Detective Johnson to report the encounter, common sense winning out over determination. The police arrived within minutes, but the strange man was already gone, nowhere to be found. Missy gave the officers a description of what he was wearing, and headed back to her shop, feeling alone and sad.

**

Sitting alone on the couch yet again, watching television, with Toffee curled up under the coffee table, Missy wished that she could talk to Chas Beckett. He'd called occasionally to check on her, even though he technically wasn't supposed to, but they confined their conversation to small talk, so he wouldn't be breaking the rules, and it just ended up making her feel even more empty. She wanted to share with him, laugh with him, and snuggle into his embrace during a movie, but she had to be content with just hearing his voice every once in a while, for now, and her patience was wearing thin.

Missy was startled when suddenly Toffee raised her head and growled a warning, looking toward the bay window in the dining room. She tapped the button on the remote control to turn the sound of her movie down, and listened as the dog continued to stare and growl into the darkness. Rising from the couch, and staying clear of the windows, Missy slipped silently into the dining room, peering out the bay window by standing beside it, so that she couldn't be seen from the outside.

The click of Toffee's claws on the restored hardwood floors rang out like gunshots in the eerie stillness of the house, as the alert animal crept slowly toward the window, head lowered. Missy strained hard to see but couldn't make anything out in the inky black evening. Toffee sat directly in front of the bay window, staring and emitting a warning growl low in her throat. On an impulse, because she couldn't stand not knowing, Missy flipped the switch for the floodlights on that side of the house, not knowing what to expect, and not disappointed when she still saw nothing. She went back to the couch, and called Toffee over, stroking her silky coat until the dog was soothed into returning to her place beneath the coffee table.

**

Missy sighed deeply, annoyed at the interruption of her regularly scheduled life.

"Well, now I know what Toffee was growling about last night," she grumbled aloud as she surveyed her car. The air had been let out of three tires, and her little burgundy car was, for the moment, immobile. She made a quick call to Ben to let him know that Cheryl would have to help him open this morning, because she was going to be late, then she called a tow-truck to have her car transported to the tire center. Happy that the air had just been released, rather than the tires themselves being destroyed, Missy pulled out of the tire center and headed for work. The entire process had taken a couple of hours, so Cheryl and Ben would still be in the midst of the morning rush when she arrived.

The Cupcake of the Day, Bittersweet Chocolate with Espresso filling and Buttery Pecan Crème topping, was quite the hit, and Missy had to pull two more trays out of the back when she arrived, jumping into the fray. Exhausted after the morning rush finally cleared around 1 p.m., she, Ben and Cheryl sat around a table in the seating area to recover for a moment before restocking.

"Whew, what a morning," Cheryl remarked, stretching her arms over her head.

"I think it's getting busier every day," Ben nodded.

"Well, when we get the LaChance store up and running again, that should thin the crowd a little bit at least," Missy mused.

They handled the handful of customers who appeared prior to closing time, then Ben and Cheryl headed home. Missy stayed at the shop to take an informal inventory, planning to attend Echo's grand opening of Sweet Love at seven o'clock. When her inventory was complete, Missy glanced at her watch, and decided to go over a bit early and beat the rush, hoping, optimistically, that there would actually be a rush. She opened the door of Sweet Love and was immediately struck by two things; first – that it smelled absolutely wonderful in the shop, and secondly, that her friend Echo was speaking with a man who had his back to the door. Echo spotted Missy and called out to her.

"Missy! Come in, come in!" she beckoned gaily, moving to the door to welcome her new friend.

The man at the counter turned around and Missy's heart sank.

"I'm sure you remember Ian," Echo said, an unreadable expression on her face.

"Yes, we've met. Look, I don't want to interrupt, I can come back later," Missy commented, backing toward the door.

"You're not interrupting at all, I was just about to fix Ian a triple cone. What would you like?" Echo asked, dragging Missy to the counter where Ian lounged insolently.

"Just a scoop of Red Chile Pepper Carob, please. To go," she added as an afterthought.

"To go? Really? I was kind of hoping that you could stick around for a bit – we can hang out and talk…"

Missy shook her head. "I really can't, I have some things I have to take care of this evening," she lied, just wanting to be on her way. "I'll take a rain check though."

"Fair enough," Echo smiled at her and ducked back behind the counter, then turned her attention to Ian, dishing up generous scoops and handing him a giant waffle cone, filled with three different flavors of frozen goodness.

"Thank you kindly," he purred at her. "You think about what I said, sugar," he winked and turned to go. "Hey, Melissa Gladstone, you need a ride home?" he teased, knowing that she clearly disapproved of him.

"No, I'm good, thanks Ian," she replied, as pleasantly as she was able. She pretended to be fascinated by the variety of flavors displayed in the glass freezer case, patently ignoring him as he sauntered from the shop. Echo dished up her treat and handed it to her in a brightly colored recycled paper bowl with a biodegradable plastic spoon.

Missy spooned a small bite of the creamy, deep brown frozen dish with tiny red flecks into her mouth and was utterly astonished. "Oh my gosh, Echo, this is amazing!" she raved, spooning up another bite. "It's rich and sweet, with just a tiny zing of heat, wow," she nodded her approval.

Echo beamed at Missy's praise. "See, I told you. I hope everyone else feels the same way."

"I'm sure they will," Missy nodded enthusiastically. "I'll do a review for you in the local paper, and let everyone know how fantastic this stuff is."

"Hey, I have an idea," the happy 'ice cream' maker said. "How about you come over on Sunday afternoon, after both of our stores close, and you can taste-test several different flavors to mention in your review?"

"Sounds fabulous and fattening," Missy mumbled through a mouthful of carob. "Count me in."

"It's a date," Echo grinned.

"Speaking of dates…it's none of my business, but it looked like you were pretty friendly toward Ian Nesbitt," Missy commented, staring intently into her ice cream bowl.

"Nah, nothing like that, he's just an ice cream lover," Echo shrugged. "What's your favorite ice cream flavor?" she changed the subject, wiping down her already spotless front counter.

"This one, so far," Missy replied, after a brief pause.

She was worried about Echo's involvement with Ian but wasn't close enough to the new gal in town to ask her outright what was going on. Maybe with time, Echo would open up.

Echo chuckled. "Well, so far, so good then."

CHAPTER SEVEN

Significant progress had been made in the rebuilding of Missy's shop in LaChance. Her contractor estimated that she might actually be able to reopen by the Thanksgiving holiday weekend, which would be perfect timing – the holidays were her busiest time of year by far. Orders flooded in beginning as early as September for holiday parties, gift boxes and baskets, and special occasions of all kinds. She had made Christmas trees out of stacked cupcakes, as well as designs that stretched across table tops for several feet. Once she knew when this location would be ready to open, she'd have to collect applications for someone to work in both the Dellville shop and the LaChance shop. She planned to have Cheryl manage the Dellville store and Ben would go back to managing the LaChance location.

The inseparable duo would be disappointed at not being able to work together anymore, but since they saw each other practically every day outside of the workplace, it wouldn't be intolerable for them.

Missy was pleased with both the progress of the LaChance shop and the performance of the Dellville shop, but everything in her life was overshadowed by the fact that Cora Nesbitt's murder was still unsolved, she was still classified as a person of interest, and she saw police cars cruising slowly by her house at times, as though keeping an eye on her. Detective Johnson had treated her report of having seen the scruffy-looking man near her shop with extreme suspicion, remarking that the sighting had certainly been 'convenient,' which infuriated Missy to no end. She had not made it up, she had really seen and chased the man, and if he had nothing to hide, why had he run?

When she parked in the back of the Dellville store, arriving early, even before Ben, Missy saw a bushel basket brimming with peaches sitting next to the back door. She unlocked the door, balancing the basket on her hip, and felt a trickle of peach juice soaking through the thin fabric of her white linen capris. Sighing, she knew that she wouldn't have a chance to go home and change, because it was Cheryl's day off and Ben couldn't handle the crowds, which would undoubtedly be showing up, on his own.

Once inside, she set the bushel basket up on the kitchen counter and grabbed a towel to try to sop up some of the peach juice on her pants. She was perplexed when she saw that the juice was tinged with red, but made the best of it, wetting the towel and trying to clean it off with a bit of dish soap. She didn't get nearly as much of the icky stain out as she would have liked, but gave up and waited for it to dry, thinking she could use stain remover before laundering them at home.

She dumped the peaches into one of the stainless steel commercial sinks so that she could wash them and dispose of the ones that had split open and were leaking juice. After emptying the basket, she glanced in the sink, her stomach doing a nauseating flip when she saw what had been hiding in the bottom of the basket. There, in the midst of the pile of plump, ripe peaches, was a severed finger, with a half-moon of dirt under the nail. Missy felt faint, but knew that this was certainly no time to swoon. She made two phone calls, the first to Ben, to let him know that he needed to call Cheryl in on her day off, the second to Detective Johnson, for obvious reasons.

Missy had requested that the police park in the rear of the building, so as not to alert customers that something was afoot, and soon, two uniformed officers, followed by Detective Johnson and a forensics tech came in the back door. The poor woman was white as a sheet, and Ben made her sit down and drink some coffee when he came in, as police swarmed her kitchen. Every time she looked down at the ugly stain on her capris and realized that there was blood mixed in with the peach juice, she had to tamp down the shuddering revulsion that rose up within her. The forensics tech swabbed her pants, and she turned her head away, not wanting to think about it.

"So what happens now?" she asked Johnson, as his team wrapped things up and prepared to leave.

"Now we test the digit for DNA, blood type, the works, we'll get a soil sample from underneath the nail, and hopefully that'll help us determine who it belongs to. We'll also be contacting local hospitals to see if anyone has come in with a missing finger. Once we find the owner of the finger, we'll be able to get more information about how it ended up in your peach basket."

"Should I be worried? Do you think this is some sort of a threat?" she asked nervously.

Johnson looked at her for a long moment before replying. "Miss Gladstone, if I find out that you somehow put the finger in the basket to throw suspicion on someone else, you should be very worried indeed."

"You think I did this?" Missy was incensed. "I am a law-abiding citizen who has done nothing wrong, and I will not have you stand there and falsely accuse me. You are welcome to leave, Detective," she directed, opening the door, eyes flashing fire and fury.

Johnson moved to the door at a leisurely pace. "Interesting that the victim's blood is on your pants," he mused, on his way out.

"I already explained how that happened, Detective. We're done here," she slammed the door shut, locking it behind him.

Missy was so overwhelmed by the ugliness of her discovery, and the rude treatment from the detective, that she quaked like a leaf, after his departure. Ben advised her to get out of the store for a while, until she recovered a bit. She had concocted a vegan poppyseed cupcake that she wanted Echo to try, so she decided to take her one and headed across the street. Echo's company would distract her and maybe, once her stomach settled a bit, she'd try another ice cream flavor.

"Hello?" Missy called out, entering the deserted shop. Echo didn't open for several hours yet but had a habit of leaving the front door unlocked.

"Back here!" she heard her friend's voice from the back room.

Wading her way past stacks of eco-friendly paper products, she wound her way to the kitchen, where Echo was on her hands and knees with a bunch of towels, mopping up a mess. Moving closer, Missy gasped.

"Echo! What happened?" she demanded, her shaking intensifying upon seeing a pool of blood seeping into the towels, the strong, coppery smell nauseating her even further.

"Clumsy me," her friend chuckled. "I spilled an entire bowl of raspberry puree. Hey…you don't look so good…why don't you have a seat up front, I'll be out shortly," she suggested, the concern in her voice evident.

Missy nodded, thankful that her original impression had been incorrect. She rationalized that she must have imagined the smell of blood after her traumatic morning. She sat at a table for two in the corner, placing the white paper bag with Echo's cupcake in it at the seat across from her. Her friend soon came bustling back into the seating area, holding a paper towel around one finger. Missy's heart nearly came out of her chest, until she noticed that the unfortunately clumsy woman still had all fingers firmly attached, she had just hurt herself somehow.

"What happened?" Missy managed to ask, hoping that she sounded somewhat normal.

"I cut myself on a can lid this morning, it's nothing really," Echo dismissed her concern with a rueful laugh and a wave. "Would you like some herbal tea? I have an organic chai that is just to die for," she offered.

"That would be nice," Missy nodded, finding Echo's word choice a bit disturbing. "I've had a rough morning. I brought you one of my new vegan creations to try," she rattled the bag, trying to be positive.

"Awesome, I'm starving!"

Echo brought their tea, and she wasn't kidding, it really was the best tea that Missy had ever tasted, and it soothed her somehow. Or, it may have just been the company of her carefree, irreverent friend that raised her spirits, but either way, she was feeling much better than when she had come over, managing to forget both about the finger in the peach basket, and the pool of raspberry puree that smelled like blood.

"Oh Missy, this cupcake is the best," Echo raved, her mouth full. "I'm seriously going to buy a hundred of them and live off of them for the next few weeks."

"Let me try some more vegan recipes before you commit to a hundred of this particular one," Missy teased, pleased that her creation was a success.

"Good idea," she nodded, still chewing. "Want to try another flavor of ice cream?" she asked gesturing to the glass fronted freezers behind them.

"Well, since you twisted my arm, I guess I'll have to," Missy smiled, standing to peer into the cases.

"Pick any one you'd like, or more than one, whatever," Echo waved breezily, still enjoying her cupcake and tea.

"Coconut Dream sounds intriguing," she pointed at a tub of snowy white frozen fluff.

"You're gonna love it!" Echo got up with a flutter of her skirt and a jangle of bracelets to dip some of the creamy concoction into a bowl for Missy, the two enjoying each other's labors of love together.

**

Chas called after Missy left Echo's shop, and despite the fact that she knew she shouldn't be discussing the Cora Nesbitt murder case with him, she had to tell him everything that had been happening to her since the murder, including her frustration with Detective Johnson.

"Don't worry about Johnson, he's always like that," Chas assured her. "Occupational hazard for some detectives."

"It's been awful, Chas," Missy confided, hating that she felt like a gossip. "They even have cars driving around my house spying on me."

"Actually, most of those times, it's probably me, doing whatever I can to watch out for you," he admitted. "But they probably have stepped up patrols as well, just in case."

"They're just barking up the wrong tree by investigating me," she muttered.

"Don't worry, Missy, they're barking up more than one tree. It may seem like nothing is moving forward with this investigation, but new evidence and more leads are discovered every day. They're getting closer."

"Don't think I'm silly for saying this, but…I miss you," she confessed, holding tightly to her phone.

There was a brief pause, causing her stomach to plummet to her knees, hoping that she hadn't said too much too soon, before Chas responded, "I know, it's frustrating…I miss you too."

Despite all of the horrific things that had happened recently, his simple admission made her heart leap, and she suddenly felt that somehow, everything would end up being okay, eventually. The two talked for another half hour or so, about daily mundane things, before hanging up with promises of a delightful reunion once the Nesbitt case was over.

CHAPTER EIGHT

Missy came back in from walking Toffee on a beautiful sunny morning and made a fresh pot of coffee, loving the way that the rich, dark, aroma scented the kitchen. Feeling better after having talked with Chas, she sighed with pleasure, basking in the sunlight of her cozy breakfast nook. Ben and Cheryl were scheduled to open this morning, so she could drink her coffee, have a leisurely breakfast while scrolling through the news on her phone, and meander in to the shop whenever she felt like it. It was the closest thing that she could get to a day off, and she intended to make the most of it. Her phone rang, interrupting her reading of a fascinating news article, and when Missy saw that it was Ben calling, she picked up immediately.

"Hey, Ms. G….so, there's something going on down here at the store," he began, sounding hesitant. "But, you probably shouldn't come down."

"What? Why? What happened, Ben?" Missy demanded, sitting up straight and reaching for her keys.

"Well, somehow, a whole lot of snakes got in here…" he sighed.

"Snakes? What do you mean snakes got in? That's impossible, there's no way for snakes to get in," Missy insisted, the hair on the back of her neck rising.

She had an unconquerable fear of the wiggly creatures. The mere thought of them caused her to tremble with dread.

"Yes ma'am, I know it's weird, but the whole place is literally crawling with snakes. Grass snakes, garter snakes, water moccasins, cotton mouths, all kinds. They're everywhere…in the cases, in the bathroom and the lounge, all over the kitchen, everywhere. I ran out of there too fast to check the freezer, but I figure they wouldn't survive in there anyway," Ben sounded a bit shaken.

Missy fought her rising hysteria. "Where are you Ben?" she asked, gritting her teeth.

"I'm outside. I got here first, so I didn't let Cheryl go in. I called Wildlife Control and they have a special team coming in to take care of it," he explained.

Shudders rippled through Missy like waves on a pond.

"Okay, good. Thank you for handling that appropriately, Ben. I'm afraid I wouldn't have been as clear-headed if I had been the one to encounter those particular circumstances."

"Yeah, I figured I'd better call and warn you so that you didn't have to see this."

"You're the best, Ben. When the Wildlife Control guys get there, you make sure that they double and triple check every inch of that shop. If I find so much as one little baby snake in my store, I will not be responsible for my actions," she warned.

"Yes ma'am, I figured that. I'll let you know when it's safe to come down, and Ms. G., we need to talk about what's going on around here."

"You're absolutely right, Ben. I value your opinion. We'll talk later today. Be careful out there," Missy said, concerned.

"I will, Ms. G., thanks."

**

The drive to Dellville was over all too soon for Missy, who was reluctant to enter her shop after having it overrun with reptiles. She loved creatures of all types, but for some reason, snakes inspired an irrational fear in her that seemed impossible to overcome. She knew that if she encountered one of the skinny, slithering critters, her reaction would be profound and embarrassing. After pulling in to her parking space, she opened the car door, looking carefully at the ground before stepping out. Summoning every ounce of courage, while her heart fluttered madly in her chest and her stomach did somersaults, she opened the back door, continually scanning every inch of the floor as she cautiously entered the kitchen. Ben was just finishing up scouring the glass cases in the front of the shop, and the image of snakes crawling through the display space that flashed through Missy's mind sent shivers up and down her spine.

"Ben, you are a saint," Missy declared, more thankful than ever for the young man's unwavering loyalty.

"At the moment, I'm a bit too smelly to be considered for sainthood," he joked, throwing a wad of paper towels into a sack that he dragged along beside him.

Pulling off his rubber gloves, he took the bag to the dumpster in the back. Missy made coffee while she waited for him to come back in and wash his hands. The shop smelled fresh and clean and showed no signs whatsoever of the creepy, crawly condition that it had been in when Ben arrived. Sitting in the sunlit eating area, it was hard to believe that the strange event had ever happened, but Missy found herself glancing in corners, nonetheless.

"Well, we lost a day of sales, but it looks like everything is taken care of and ready to go for tomorrow," Ben observed, sitting down across from his boss.

Missy rubbed her temples. "This just keeps getting weirder and weirder, Ben."

"Yeah, it does," he agreed, standing and moving to the kitchen to pour their coffee when he heard the burbling of the brewer stop. "Do you think that all of this stuff is being done on purpose?" he asked, setting down a mug in front of her and sipping from his own.

"Well, clearly it's on purpose, there's been too much going on to be passed off as mere coincidence, but why? Why would someone do this?" Her question wasn't rhetorical, she really wanted an objective and educated opinion. Ben was a grad student in Criminal Justice and had an insight into both criminals and the justice system that she did not.

"Let's just take a look at events…Ms. G., you've had nothing but trouble ever since you bought this place. It makes me wonder if it's haunted or something," Ben sighed in exasperation.

"Well, thanks for that extremely scientific analysis, Ben," Missy teased. "But I'll remind you that I did not get where I am today by being a shrinking violet who runs at the first sign of trouble."

"I know, I get that, and I'm not saying to give up, but I'm worried about you. A severed finger? A heaping helping of snakes? These events have gone from being symbolically threatening to actually threatening, and I'm guessing that if Detective Dufus

Johnson doesn't catch whoever is doing it, that things will continue to escalate."

"He's only investigating this case because he thinks I'm connected to Cora Nesbitt's murder somehow. He thinks I'm making these events happen to throw him off or something," Missy grimaced. "Speaking of the dear detective, how did it go when he showed up?"

Ben shook his head in disgust. "He didn't get here until after Wildlife Control had already finished the roundup, so he treated me like I was being hysterical over the fact that somehow a couple of snakes had gotten in."

Missy absently patted down the hackles that had risen on the back of her neck, then unconsciously rubbed the goosebumps on her arms.

"How many snakes were there, exactly?" she asked, dreading the answer.

"WC said over a hundred. They didn't get an exact count because some of them were picked up in tangled clumps."

Closing her eyes against the nausea rising in the back of her throat, Missy tried to erase the image that Ben had just described from her mind. "Did Johnson talk to the WC guys?"

"He said that he would follow up with them, but who knows?"

Missy twirled her coffee mug round and round, thinking. "I just can't help but wonder who would do this, and why. I don't have any enemies that I know of," she shrugged, feeling helpless and confused.

"I think I might have an idea about that," Ben said slowly.

She sat forward. "Who? Who is it?"

"Cheryl and I have both seen the hippie-looking guy, who pretended to dislike your lemon cupcake so that he'd get it for free, wandering around down here.

Sometimes he'll stand just out of sight between two buildings, and when we go out to confront him, he disappears."

"But why would this total stranger, no matter how creepy he seems, have any interest in scaring me away? It just doesn't make sense," Missy shook her head, frustrated.

"Yeah, I haven't figured that out yet, but, believe me, if I get a chance to confront this dude, I plan on getting some answers," Ben vowed grimly.

"Just be careful. I don't need to be worried about your safety too," she patted his hand.

CHAPTER NINE

Missy sat with Echo in Sweet Love, a spoon and samplers of seven different kinds of frozen delights placed in front of her. She had told her friend about the episode with the snakes and was surprised when the free-spirited woman had giggled.

"What on earth is funny about an entire shop full of snakes?" Missy asked, tasting a lovely vanilla bean, soy milk ice cream.

"The unwarranted prejudice against those beautiful creatures just never ceases to amaze me," Echo frowned. "Why on earth would a store full of snakes be any more intimidating than a store full of bunnies? They're no more dangerous. I have a few of them myself," she replied, pushing a container of a light, yellowish-orange colored treat in front of her to try next.

"Ewww…you have snakes in your house…by choice?" Missy was astounded, her spoon stopping midway to her mouth.

"They're pets. Watch out, you're going to drip," she looked pointedly at the spoon, which Missy then popped into her mouth.

"Oh wow, that's delicious, it tastes like fresh-picked peaches," she exclaimed. "And I just think it's strange to voluntarily house reptiles."

"You have a dog, it's all the same," Echo asserted firmly. "That's my rice milk peach whip. Ian Nesbitt had more peaches from his aunt's trees than he had buyers for, so he brought me several bushels and they just have the best flavor.

Missy exercised a great deal of willpower in not grimacing at the mention of Ian's name, preferring to focus on the delightful dessert in front of her.

"Hey, you know what…Ian Nesbitt is actually the reason that I'm afraid of snakes," she remembered.

"Ian? How on earth did that come about?" Echo asked, presenting the next concoction, a Honduran coffee ice cream made with coconut milk.

"He was a couple of years behind me in school, and when I was in seventh grade, on the last day of school, he slipped a garter snake into my backpack. I opened it up at home, in my room, and reached in, startling the snake, and it latched onto the webbing between my thumb and forefinger. I pulled my hand out of the backpack and shook it as hard as I could, flinging the snake to the floor and ran from my room screaming. I refused to go back into my room until my dad went in and removed the snake. I had nightmares for weeks after that, and found out from Ian that he was the nasty little prankster who did it. I didn't speak to him for quite a while," Missy shuddered, remembering. She took a bite of the coffee treat and her eyes practically rolled back in her head at the ridiculously delicious flavor.

Echo stifled a giggle behind her hand. "Well, you can't exactly blame the snake in that scenario. Sounds like Ian was quite the little mischief maker back in the day."

"Mischief...hmmf, that's one word for it," Missy observed wryly.

"Don't you think he's kinda cute?" Echo asked casually.

"Cute? Ian? Hardly. I'm actually shocked that you do," Missy raised an eyebrow.

"Really? Why? He's good looking, charming, has that 'Southern boy manners' thing going on," she sighed. "I mean...wow. Why wouldn't I think he was wonderful? My first impression of him was clearly all wrong. I don't know what I was thinking, but I'm glad he came back, so that I could see what he's really like."

Missy put down her spoon, trying hard not to let the degree of her distaste for Ian Nesbitt show when she answered. "Hmm...I don't know, maybe because he's a spoiled little conspicuous consumer who has never worked a day in his life and you're setting out to save the planet one recycled bowl at a time?"

"You really don't like him, do you?" Echo observed.

"I actually don't really care one way or the other. I hadn't thought about him in years before I ran into him after his aunt's death. We're just very different people I suppose," Missy shrugged as a bowl of light green ice cream was placed in front of her. "What's this one?" she asked, poking at the mass with her spoon.

"Ginger and lime," Echo responded, still focused on their conversation. "Well, you and I are very different people, and we get along well."

"Yes we do, and I'm glad," Missy smiled, taking a bite of the latest treat. "Oooooo! This is made with coconut milk too, isn't it?"

Her friend beamed. "Yup, put the lime in the coconut and eat it all up!" she joked.

The two laughed and chatted and found themselves forgetting all about snakes and Ian Nesbitt as they discussed everything from the environment to politics to old boyfriends. Echo became markedly distant when that topic came up, making vague references to shiftless charlatans, and Missy made a mental note to ask her more later. When Missy left a couple of hours later, stuffed and happy, she was thankful for a pleasant afternoon, and was looking forward to exercising her ice cream indulgence away in the company of her lovable and enthusiastic Toffee.

**

Missy sat on her couch, an unopened novel on the seat beside her, absently stroking Toffee's fluffy ears and thinking about Chas. She missed his smile and easygoing manner. He had a way of making even the darkest of days seem at least a bit brighter. The more that she thought about the ridiculous situation that was separating her from the handsome detective, the more frustrated she became, finally making up her mind to call him, come what may.

"I miss you," Chas said, without preamble when he answered her call.

Missy's heart beat faster at the sound of his voice, and his kind words were a balm to her weary soul. "I miss you too, and I have an idea."

"That sounds like something that could get me in trouble," he teased.

"Not at all," she reassured him, fingers crossed behind her back. "I'm going to be having a dish of ice cream at Sweet Love in Dellville tomorrow, around four o'clock. If you, coincidentally, happened to have a craving for ice cream at that same time and wind up in the same place, surely there's nothing wrong with that, right?" she asked innocently, with just a touch of mischief in her voice.

"Actually, it stretches the bounds of propriety, but, whatever. I haven't had ice cream in ages, so yes, there is a good chance that I might be hungry for a monster cone around four o'clock tomorrow," he replied, and Missy could hear the smile in his voice.

"Well, I will warn you in advance…Sweet Love is an entirely different kind of ice cream shop," she chuckled, delighted at the thought of finally seeing him.

"Different? Different how?" he asked, his suspicion aroused.

"Let's just say, it's a healthier alternative than the typical ice cream place."

"Healthy and ice cream should not be in the same sentence. I don't indulge in dessert often, but when I do, I'm perfectly okay with the fact that I'm shoveling an artery-hardening caloric nightmare into my mouth," Chas grumbled.

Missy laughed. "Don't worry, I've tasted several varieties, and I think your preference for decadent dessert will be more than satisfied," she assured him.

"Actually, I probably won't even know what flavor I'm eating, I'll be too busy paying attention to one of my fellow patrons."

Blushing, despite the fact that he couldn't see the impact of his words on her, Missy enjoyed the rest of their brief conversation and hung up feeling relieved. Immediately after hanging up, she rushed upstairs to her closet to find the perfect outfit for the next day, finally settling upon a bright fuchsia knit dress with a sweetheart neckline. Choosing simple white beads and strappy sandals to complete the look, she hung the outfit on the back of the bathroom door so that she could slip into it after her shower in the morning.

CHAPTER TEN

Morning dawned grey and dreary, with a light drizzle that did little more than raise the humidity, making the heat seem oppressive, but Missy didn't care. She sailed through her morning routine, leaving the house ten minutes earlier than usual. The workday sped past with a bustling crowd keeping her, and Cheryl, busy right up until lunchtime. After the glass cases were restocked, and all prep was done for the next day, Missy let the hard-working young lady head out early, confident that she could handle any customers straggling in on her own. She had just tipped the last of the chairs upside down on a table, officially closing the shop for the day, when she spotted the scruffy-looking man, who had run from her before, slipping into an alley next to the ice cream shop across the street. She couldn't leave the store unattended to chase after him, by the time she ran to the back for her keys to lock the door, he would be gone, and she might be putting herself in danger if she provoked him again, so, in utter frustration, she watched as he disappeared yet again, not bothering to even call Detective Johnson.

The cloudy greyness of the day apparently had a negative impact upon the flow of business at Sweet Love, because when Missy went over at 3:55, watching anxiously for Chas's car, the only person in the store was Echo, who sat at one of the tables reading a magazine.

"Slow day?" Missy asked, beaming at her friend.

"Crazy slow!" Echo nodded. "How bout you?"

"No, we were as busy as ever, although it really dropped off in the afternoon."

"Are you here for a visit or can I get you something?" she closed the magazine.

"Both, actually, and there's someone I want you to meet, when he gets here," Missy added shyly.

"Look at you blushing," Echo teased. "He must be really special."

"He definitely is…" Missy began, closing her mouth when the object of her affection and conversation walked in the door.

"Well, imagine running into you here – what a coincidence," Chas grinned at her, brushing her lips briefly with his.

Missy resisted the urge to cling to him and observed the proper decorum for two people who weren't supposed to be seeing each other.

"What a coincidence indeed," she agreed, glowing. "There's someone I want you to meet."

She took him by the hand, practically dragging him over to where Echo had risen out of her chair, and introduced the two, forgetting to mention that Chas was a detective.

"So you're the new owner here, congratulations," he said, extending his hand, which she shook briefly.

"Thanks, it's been quite the adventure," Echo's gaze traveled subtly from head to toe over the handsome detective.

"Are you from around here?" he asked, while moving over in front of the freezer cases to check out the selection.

"No, I just moved here," she replied, going to stand behind the counter, because the dashing man was clearly interested in getting some dessert. Missy moved to his side, ostensibly to check out the current flavors, but clearly just trying to find any reason at all to be next to Chas.

"Really? Where from?" Chas peered more closely into the freezer case.

"California. See something you'd like?" she asked coyly.

Missy completely missed the double entendre, entirely preoccupied with deciding between Carrot Bran Coconut Dream, which tasted just like carrot cake, and Banana with Carob Chips, but Chas picked up the subtle signal immediately and chose to ignore it.

"I'd like to try the Peanut Butter Parfait please, just two scoops in a dish," he answered, pretending that he hadn't received the very clear invitation. "So, what brings you all the way to the swamps of the deep South from California?" he asked innocently.

"Change of scenery," was the terse reply, delivered with a somewhat strained smile that Detective Beckett's acute perception didn't miss. "Missy, what'll you have?" Echo turned her attention away from the detective, who continued to observe her.

"I think I'm going to go with the Carrot Bran," she decided finally, craving carrot cake. She'd have to whip up a batch of Spiced Carrot Cupcakes in the morning and top them with ooey gooey cream cheese and pecan frosting.

"Good choice," she commented, dipping a large scoop into a bowl for her friend. "Hey, if you guys don't mind, I have some things to take care of in the back. Help yourself to water or anything else that you might need, okay?"

"Okay, we'll go have a seat on the patio if you finish up and want to join us," Missy replied, puzzled. She had been so eager to introduce Chas to her new friend, and now Echo just disappeared. The couple carried their bowls to a bistro table on the patio, enjoying the fresh air from underneath the table's umbrella, despite the cloudy weather.

Chas seemed to be deep in thought. "How long have you two known each other?" he asked conversationally.

"Just since she bought the shop, not very long at all. We just seemed to bond really quickly."

"So why do you think she moved here from California?" he was suddenly very interested in his ice cream, avoiding Missy's eyes while she answered.

"You know, it's kind of strange, I've asked her that myself, multiple times, but she never really seems to answer. I get the impression that it may have had something to do with a failed relationship, but I'm not sure."

Chas nodded, savoring a bite of Peanut Butter Parfait. "Just seems a little weird that someone who is so clearly into a very 'California' lifestyle would pull up stakes and move to a teeny tiny town in Louisiana to run a vegan ice cream store. I wonder how she got the money for the purchase…Did she have an ice cream store out there that she sold?" he asked, lowering his voice.

"Hmmm…you know, she never said. I have no idea. For all I know, she could be a bank robber," Missy giggled. Chas chuckled along, but his smile didn't quite reach his eyes.

**

Detective Chas Beckett had a feeling in his gut that all was not as it seemed in regard to Echo Willis. He had a good friend who was a detective in the LAPD, and he pulled some strings to have him run a check on her. His friend, Chuck Grambino, said that he would do what he could and get back to him in a couple of days. In the meantime, Chas was going to do some checking of his own and see what he came up with. It bothered him tremendously that Missy seemed to take the woman at face value, but he didn't want to warn her off if there was really nothing sinister in her past or present.

Feeling restless, he decided to park his unmarked car behind a building that gave him a perfect vantage point for watching the back door of Sweet Love. Every other shop in the area had been closed for hours, but there were still lights on in the back of Echo's store. A large, solid panel van pulled up close to the back door and a man got out. Chas was too far away to see any distinguishing features, but could tell that he was somewhat tall, around 6', of medium build, and wore dark-colored clothing. The man looked around before dashing into the building, then came back out shortly thereafter carrying a bulky, obviously heavy bundle. Beckett had seen bundles like that before, and if it was what he thought it was, his intuition regarding Echo Willis had been correct.

When the van left Sweet Love, it turned the corner right before the block where Chas was sitting in his car, giving him a perfect line of sight to the license plate. Copying down the number, he followed the van with his lights off, disappearing against the backdrop of the darkened city streets, but once he came to a more populated area, he dropped back further, so as not to be seen, and lost the van at a stoplight. Instead of heading home, he headed to the station, Chas Beckett had work to do.

CHAPTER ELEVEN

Missy was disconcerted to say the least, when she awoke to a loud banging on her front door. Hurriedly, she slipped into her robe and glanced at the time on her cell phone. Who on earth would be at her door at 6:30 in the morning? Toffee had practically leapt from her plaid fluffy bed in the corner of Missy's room, and charged down the stairs ahead of her human. Sighing aloud when she looked through the peephole and saw Detective Gilbert Johnson accompanied by two uniformed officers, Missy unlatched the chain and opened the door.

"Ms. Gladstone, sorry to bother you at this hour, but I have a few questions for you, if you don't mind," the detective explained.

"Do we have to do this now?" Missy sighed, not wanting to conduct any kind of interview in her robe.

"Time is of the essence, I'm afraid," Johnson insisted.

"Fine," Missy opened the door to let him in. "Please have a seat at the kitchen table. I'm going to go get dressed and I'll be back down in two minutes."

"Not a problem," he nodded, taking a seat. The uniforms remained standing.

Missy returned, clad simply in light blue capris and a white polo shirt, with her hair atop her head in a messy bun. "I'm going to make coffee while we chat, would you like some?" she asked, measuring the grounds into a filter.

"No, thank you."

"Would you boys like a cup?" she offered to the two uniforms standing silently in the dining room. Both said no, but seemed pleased to have been asked.

"What brings you here this time, Detective?" she asked, pouring water into the coffee maker.

"Can you verify your whereabouts last night?"

Here we go again with the interrogations, she thought, making an effort not to sound as irritated as she felt.

"I was asked to provide three different types of cupcakes for the Methodist Church New Member Social, so I stayed to meet the new folks, and chatted with Sally Helgerson, the Pastor's wife until around nine o'clock, then I came home and cleaned the cupcake trays that are sitting to the left of the sink over there," she gestured to the trays that were in full view, sitting on a drying rack. "After that, I went to bed, and was actually exhausted enough that I fell asleep immediately."

"That's what I'd heard from Bonnie, down at the station. She was at the social last night. Just wanted to confirm it with you. Sally Helgerson corroborated that account, and so did your neighbor across the street, who was sitting on her front porch and noticed both when you came home and when your lights went out," Johnson nodded, making a note in his notebook, then closing it.

"Detective, why is where I was last night so important that you'd come over just after sunrise to ask me about it? Particularly when you'd heard where I was from multiple people," Missy asked, puzzled.

The detective looked pained, almost as if he'd eaten something that didn't quite agree with him. "We...found something, and we thought that you might possibly be involved."

"Really? What was it that you found?" she sat down, her hands wrapped around a cup of fresh coffee.

"A body," he said, watching her for a reaction.

Missy put down her mug, eyes wide with surprise. "A body? Oh dear...who is it?" she asked, not certain that she wanted to hear the answer.

"Well, actually we were hoping that you might be able to help us determine that."

"Me? How on earth could I help you determine the identity of a body?" she was horrified at the thought.

"The description of the individual closely matches the description that you gave us of the drifter who scammed free cupcakes from you and used your phone to call Cora Nesbitt before she died. I'd like you to come down to the morgue and take a look to see if you think it's the same person."

Missy shuddered at the thought, the hair on the back of her neck standing up. Swallowing hard, she said, "Well, if you think it would help, I could try. Do you think he's the one who killed Mrs. Nesbitt?"

"We're still conducting an investigation, it would be inappropriate for me to comment on the case at this time," he said formally.

"Of course, I understand," Missy said softly, overwhelmed. "I don't have to go now, do I? I'd really love to have a shower before I leave the house, if that's okay."

"That's perfectly fine," the detective stood to go. "Take your time getting ready and give me a call when you leave. I'll meet you at the morgue. The identification process should be fairly quick," he reassured her. It was the nicest he'd ever been since she met him, and she wondered if they were finally close to solving the case and realizing that she'd had no part in Cora Nesbitt's death.

Missy moved through her morning routine in a daze, shaken to the core by the news of yet another death, even if it was the death of a stranger. She showered, took Toffee for a short walk, and called Detective Johnson to let him know that she was headed for the morgue. When she pulled into the hospital parking lot, a wave of revulsion shook her at the thought of having to identify a corpse. She took several deep breaths, walked into the main entrance of the hospital, and took the elevator to the basement, as Johnson had instructed her to do when she called. By the time she stepped out of the elevator, the detective was already there, waiting for her with a very serious look on his face. With Johnson stood the coroner's assistant, wearing rubber gloves and holding a small, white jar. The detective greeted her in a subdued manner, and, taking the small jar from the coroner's assistant, opened it, dipped a finger in and rubbed a strongly minty-smelling substance under his nose, coating his upper lip.

"You'll want to do the same," he said, holding the jar out to Missy.

"Why?" she recoiled a bit at the heavy, medicinal smell.

The coroner's assistant stepped forward and explained gently, "It's for the smell. The body has not yet been embalmed, so there are certain odors present that most people find more than a little unpleasant."

"Isn't there, like, glass to stand behind, where I look at the…deceased from a window or something?"

Missy asked, her eyes darting from the coroner to the detective.

"Our facility isn't equipped for that," the coroner replied, glancing at his watch.

Missy cringed, wanting very much to turn and flee from this depressing place and uncomfortable situation, but instead, dipped her fingers in just like Johnson had done, and spread the oily jelly under her nose. The assistant closed the jar and turned to lead the way into a postmortem examination room. "Aren't you going to use any?" Missy asked.

"After seeing several hundred, one gets accustomed to it," the assistant answered quietly, opening the door to a brightly lit room, which still seemed somehow dark, where a human form rested beneath an industrial green sheet. Missy stayed behind the woman from the coroner's office, not wanting to get any closer to the body.

"Ms. Gladstone, would you step over here please?" Detective Johnson spoke, gesturing for her to come and stand beside him. Despite her extreme reluctance, Missy did as he asked, positioning herself near the head of the examination table.

The coroner's assistant stood at the other side of the table, directly across from her, and looked at Missy. "Ready?" she asked, holding the corner of the sheet in her gloved hand. Missy shook her head, but Johnson said, 'Yes' in a manner that caused the woman to fold the sheet back, exposing the face of the dead man. Missy gasped, her hand going to her mouth as she recognized the stranger who had been hanging around her shop. Overcome, she ran from the room and leaned weakly against the wall of the corridor, dry heaving and crying. When Detective Johnson came out to check on her, she held her hand out, unable to speak, horrified.

"Do you recognize that man?" he asked quietly.

Missy nodded, swallowing convulsively.

"Was this the man who came into your store and called Cora Nesbitt?" he persisted.

She nodded again, recovering a bit, but still not quite herself. "Yes, it was," she whispered.

"Okay," he nodded. "Thank you Ms. Gladstone. Take as much time as you need – whenever you feel up to it, you're free to go."

"Thank you," Missy replied weakly, moving slowly toward the elevator, holding on to the wall for support, desperately wanting to get as far away from this place as possible.

CHAPTER TWELVE

Detective Chas Beckett stared hard at the report that had been faxed to him by his contact in California. According to the report, there was no such person as Echo Willis, but the name had been used as an alias by a woman reportedly trying to start a new life after a dangerous run-in with some very unsavory individuals. The woman had been a junior executive with a well-known company in Silicon Valley, and had been dating a man, Albert Jenkins, who, unbeknownst to her, was associated with local drug distributors. Albie Jenkins had played the part of high roller a little too well, and she had gotten serious enough about the man to have moved in with him, the two of them enjoying the domestic bliss of a 7000 square foot home on the beach with an indoor/outdoor pool, until the day that she discovered that the love of her life had a very wicked temper and was not afraid to work out his frustrations with his fists.

Her story was that she had tried to run, but Jenkins had kept her captive until some professional thugs came in to put him in his place because of massive debts owed to their boss. They roughed up the boyfriend badly enough that she seized her opportunity to escape, leaving the beaten man alive, but penniless, homeless and without a clue as to the whereabouts of his former love. The thing that didn't add up for Chas was the total change in the woman's persona. It was more than odd for a former business executive to suddenly adopt the lifestyle of a 'life-on-the-fringe' free-spirited bohemian who decided to move to Louisiana on a whim. Although, if she were trying to erase her former identity in order to not be found, she had gone about it in brilliant fashion, moving to a small obscure town and adopting a personality that was the furthest that one could get from what she had been. The woman's real name, before she took the moniker 'Echo Willis,' was Constance Evans. Beckett had every intention of keeping an eye on her and finding out what she was really doing in Dellville, Louisiana.

**

"I had a date last night," Echo confessed, delighted, when Missy came over for a rice cream 'milkshake,' a few days after her disturbing visit to the morgue. She hadn't told anyone but Chas about it, and he felt that it was probably best that way.

"Really? That's great! With whom?" Missy asked, digging into her Vanilla Bean Rice Cream Milkshake.

"Ian Nesbitt," she announced proudly, as her friend cringed inwardly.

"Ah. That's…nice. What did you two do?"

She didn't actually want to know, finding it difficult to believe that anyone could last for more than two minutes in the company of the obnoxious trust-fund boy, but was trying to sound interested for Echo's sake.

"We went out to dinner at this cute little place called the Crawshack Redemption, do you know it?" she asked.

Missy swallowed a huge amount of ice cream, driving ice picks of pain through her brain. "I've heard of it," she said vaguely, wanting to change the subject. She had some very unpleasant memories about the Crawshack Redemption, and even though it was under new ownership, the very thought of it made her anxious. "What did you do after dinner?"

"He took me to the house that he inherited from his aunt, and talked about all the ways he's going to improve both the house and the land. He has such big plans and is so excited about the possibilities."

"Echo, you do realize that the reason he inherited that house is because his aunt was murdered, right?" Missy was appalled at the thought that dear Mrs.

Nesbitt hadn't even cooled in her grave yet and Ian was already mentally moving into her home. The man had no soul.

"Yeah, it's so sad, he showed me the exact spot where she died."

"Really? Didn't you think that was a little odd for a first date?"

"I try not to judge people, Missy. It was obviously on his mind, and he doesn't seem to have anyone to talk with about it," Echo shrugged it off.

Suddenly Missy no longer wanted her rice milkshake. "Yeah, I could see how that would happen," she said softly, wanting to end the conversation. "Thanks for the shake, I've got to run. You should stop by the shop tomorrow, it's Mango Madness Vegan Cupcake day."

"Sounds good," Echo gave her a confused smile, wondering about the change in her demeanor and sudden eagerness to exit. "I'll definitely see you in the morning."

**

"Chas, I don't care what anyone thinks, I need to talk to you, sooner rather than later," Missy told the handsome detective on the phone, after her conversation with Echo.

"Not a problem, pretty lady, I have some things that I want to share with you too," Beckett replied.

"Can you just come over?" she was a bit embarrassed at the need in her voice.

"I think it's probably best if we meet somewhere else. There's a little tavern off of route 27 about 6 miles out of town…" he began.

"Off a dirt road, tucked in behind an abandoned carriage house? Yeah, I know it. When should I head over there?" Missy interrupted, eager to see him.

"Ten minutes?"

"Perfect, I'll see you then."

Despite the fact that Missy was meeting Chas in order to share what might just turn out to be important information regarding Cora Nesbitt's murder, she was still looking forward to being in the comfort of his presence, and changed into a fresh outfit, wanting to look her best.

Two good ol' boys were bellied up to the bar at the Pit Stop tavern, where a hard-bitten woman with dyed blue-black hair, and a stare that could frost a flirtatious man's soul, was tending bar, and country music whined dully in the background. Chas told Missy to grab a table in the corner, where they'd be out of sight and out of mind, giving them privacy from anyone who might've noticed their existence. He returned to the table with a club soda for himself and a sweet tea for Missy.

"Hitting the hard stuff tonight?" she teased, when she saw him with a soda.

"Guilty pleasure," he grinned boyishly. "So, what's got you all aflutter this evening?" Chas asked, gazing into her eyes in a manner that warmed her from head to toe.

"I had a rather disturbing conversation with Echo that I think might be important."

"Disturbing? Disturbing how?" suddenly, he was all business.

"Well, she said that she had a date with Ian Nesbitt, Cora Nesbitt's nephew. After he took her to dinner, he gave her a tour of Cora's house that he inherited, and here's the weird thing…she said that he pointed out to her the exact place that Cora died."

Chas sat back, frowning. "Go on," he encouraged, listening intently.

"How could he have known that information, Chas? Word around town is that he didn't find his aunt's body, her housekeeper did. The police aren't giving that kind of information to the news people, which means, I hate to say this, but the only way that Ian

Nesbitt could've known the precise spot where his aunt had died…"

"…Is if he was the one who killed her," the detective finished the thought. "That could very well be the missing link in the evidence," he said, light dawning.

"Missing link?" Missy was confused.

"Although I wasn't allowed to personally conduct any of the investigation on the case, due to my connection with you, Detective Johnson brought me in to help sort through the evidence and try to make some sense of what was going on. He knew that I wouldn't be biased in my assessment, even if it ultimately implicated you, and he needed an extra set of eyes. After meeting your friend, Echo, something about her just didn't seem to be adding up, so I had a law enforcement buddy of mine in California do some digging and found out that the name Echo Willis was an alias, and that she had fled the state to escape a very abusive ex-boyfriend, who had ties to drug dealers and other assorted thugs."

Missy's eyes widened. "Echo came to Louisiana to hide?"

"Apparently," Chas nodded. "And unfortunately, she didn't cover her tracks well enough. Jenkins found her and has been stalking her for weeks."

"What? He's here? Oh my goodness, is Echo in danger?" Missy worried.

"Not any longer. The body you identified in the morgue was Albert Jenkins."

It took a moment for Missy to register the full impact of Chas's words, and when they sunk in, she felt faint and a bit nauseated. Dropping her head into her hands, she tried to puzzle out all of the implications. "So, the homeless guy that I gave a cupcake to was really a bad guy who followed Echo out here from California?"

Chas nodded.

"So, then…did he actually kill Mrs. Nesbitt?"

"All of the evidence had been pointing in that direction. The fingerprints that he left on your phone, were a match to those left at Cora Nesbitt's home. He was nowhere to be found after the murder, but you and Ben both saw him lurking about in the general vicinity of the ice cream shop on more than one occasion. There was a foul-smelling substance on his clothing when he died, and when we tested it, the lab came back with a very unusual result."

"What was it?" Missy asked, breathless.

"Snake feces. Apparently, Mr. Jenkins was the man who wrangled all of the snakes that were dumped into your shop. It turns out that one of his money-laundering businesses for the drug trade out in California had been a pet shop specializing in reptiles. He'd had experience in handling even the most venomous of snakes and had apparently used them on more than one occasion to snuff out competitors in his particular line of work but walked free because it couldn't be proven."

Missy shuddered at the thought of death by snake. "So, when you say that Ian Nesbitt provided the missing link in the evidence, what did you mean?"

"Well, despite the fact that Albert Jenkins was a verified bad guy, who had definitely been in the wrong place at the wrong time, there were a few things that didn't quite add up. The first and most obvious is motive. What reason could he possibly have to kill Mrs. Nesbitt? It made no sense, particularly if he was trying to maintain a low profile while he stalked his ex-girlfriend. Secondly, there was physical evidence that just didn't fit."

"Like what?"

"Like the finger that was in your peach basket. It belonged to Albert Jenkins. If he were the one making threats, why would he cut off his own finger to do it? We did scrapings of the material under the nail on the severed finger and found DNA samples that didn't match his, almost as if there had been a struggle and he had scratched his adversary. At the crime scene, there was a heavy pewter candle-stick that the killer had used to strike Mrs. Nesbitt in the back of the head before pushing her down the stairs to make it look like an accident. There were fingerprints on the candlestick that didn't match Albert's, yours, or the housekeeper's. We ran them through the national database and came up empty," Chas explained.

"Then there's the matter of Albert turning up dead. I had staked out Sweet Love and saw a man pull up in a van after hours, go into the shop and come out shortly thereafter with a very large bundle. A body-sized bundle. I followed the van as closely as I could without being detected but lost it in traffic once I got into a more populated area. I would bet that Albert had gone to the ice cream shop to lie in wait for Echo, and Ian followed him there to kill him. We're still waiting for the autopsy to come back, so we'll know more soon. My guess is that when we test the DNA that was under Albert Jenkins' nails and compare the fingerprints on the candlestick with those of Ian Nesbitt, we'll have our murderer."

"But why would Ian kill his own aunt? I mean, I may think he's a terrible human being, but she was his only living relative and she was always kind to him. And why, after that, would he kill Albert Jenkins, a stranger in town?" Missy was perplexed.

"You said yourself that Ian was a spoiled, entitled man, living off of his inheritance. I'm going to do some checking into his finances, but I would bet that he's close to running out of money. Cora Nesbitt's home, land and assets are considerable, and as her only living relative, Ian gets everything when she dies. It's horrible to think about, but Ian may have planned to do this for quite some time, and seized the opportunity when a drifter came to town that he could frame for the murder."

"How do you explain the severed finger?" Missy grimaced.

"Putting two and two together, I'd say that Ian probably saw Jenkins in the house before he went out to the orchard to pick peaches, and killed his aunt after Albert left. He most likely then went out to where Jenkins was working and offered him a considerable amount of money to buy his silence. Jenkins accepted the deal, and Ian somehow had the notion that he was then in control of the drifter. He didn't know that Albert had an agenda."

"Why would Ian have cut off Albert's finger though?"

"That may have been entirely personal. Jenkins had come all the way from California because of Echo, and Ian has clearly been interested in her from the first time he met her. I think Ian found out the real reason that the drifter had come to town and probably wanted to let Albert know that he was in control and would take drastic measures to keep him in his place. Men have done stranger things to protect the woman they love," Chas' innocent comment made Missy blush, and she looked away. "Using the finger to scare you was just a bonus that Ian hadn't counted on but enjoyed after you rejected him pretty soundly a couple of times. In his twisted mind, he probably saw it as a harmless prank."

"Do you think the snakes were a prank as well?"

"Doubtful. I think Jenkins probably did that one on his own because he saw your growing relationship with Echo as a threat, and he may have been exacting revenge because you recognized him loitering and chased him down the street."

"Do you think Ian is a danger to Echo?" Missy worried.

"Probably not. I think Echo just makes very poor choices when it comes to the men in her life," Chas shook his head. "Well, sweet Missy, as much as I'd love to stay and chat with the most beautiful woman in Lausanne Parish, I need to get to the office and call Johnson in to brief him on all of this so that we can bring Ian Nesbitt in for questioning."

"I can't wait until all of this is over and we can go back to living our normal lives," Missy said, reaching for his hand as he stood to go.

"That makes two of us," Chas agreed, leaning down to kiss her. "But then again, when is life ever normal?"

CHAPTER THIRTEEN

Missy called Echo twice the next day, just to chat, and was a bit concerned when her friend didn't answer the phone, so she planned to walk over to Sweet Love once traffic at her own shop slowed down a bit in the afternoon. Heading across the street around 3:30, she was surprised to find Echo's helper, a high school gal named Donna, standing outside in front of the ice cream shop.

"Hi Donna," Missy smiled. "What are you doing out here in the heat?"

"I showed up for my shift a few minutes ago, but Miss Willis isn't here yet. She must be running late or something," the teenager mused, scrolling through text messages on her phone.

"Hmm...that's odd. Echo is usually here well in advance of opening time," Missy frowned, pulling her phone out of her back pocket.

She tried Echo's number again, still no answer. Her next call was an urgent one to Chas Beckett. Walking around the side of the shop to have some privacy, she dialed his number.

"Chas," she exclaimed when he answered. "I've been trying to reach Echo all day, and she's not answering her phone, and now she's not here to open Sweet Love, I think something may be terribly, terribly wrong," she spoke urgently into the receiver, trying to keep her voice down.

"Echo is safe, but it's a long story that I don't have time to go into right now," the detective assured her, sounding distracted. "I'll call you tonight to explain. You can go ahead and send Donna home, the shop won't be opening today."

**

Missy hugged her pale and shaken friend when she appeared on her doorstep, looking bedraggled and tired.

"Echo, oh my goodness, I've been so worried about you, please come in."

She led the somewhat dazed woman to the couch, and once she was seated, tenderhearted Toffee came over and gently laid her head on the distressed woman's knee, peering up at her with sad brown eyes. The dog's kindness was her undoing, and Echo burst into tears, reaching down to bury her face in Toffee's fur as she cried, her arms around the dog's neck.

Missy sat down beside her and put her arm around Echo's shaking shoulders, letting her cry into Toffee's silken fur, having done exactly that on several occasions lately. When her sobs eased a bit and she sat up, wiping her face, Missy gave her a huge hug.

"I'm going to make you some tea and serve up a Mango Madness cupcake for you, you look like you could use a snack," she observed kindly, handing Echo a tissue.

"I don't want to be any trouble," her friend replied weakly.

"Oh honey, you're in the South now, this is what we do," Missy smiled.

Echo stroked Toffee's silky ears. The sensitive animal stayed by her side, seeming to know the simple comfort that she was providing. Missy puttered around in the kitchen, coming back moments later with a delicious, fluffy cupcake and a hot cup of tea, placing them on the coffee table in front of her friend.

"Darlin, what happened to you?" she asked, brushing a tangle of auburn curls away from Echo's face.

"Oh, Missy, it was awful," she bit her lip. "So...I told you how excited I was that I had a date with Ian Nesbitt," she began.

143

Missy's stomach lurched at the sound of his name, now that she knew that he had most likely murdered not only his aunt, but Echo's creepy ex-boyfriend as well.

"Yes, I remember," Missy said, careful to not let her revulsion show.

"Well, he picked me up for a lunch date and he was, I don't know, agitated. So I asked him what was wrong, and he started yelling about how he had found out that one of my ex-boyfriends was in town and how I should've told him and then he started talking crazy, saying how he had not only taken care of it, but how he had enjoyed it. I got really scared and told him that I wanted to go home, but he refused to turn around, saying that I was his now, and that I had to do whatever he told me to do. He drove really fast and recklessly and I didn't know what was going to happen. Oh Missy, it was so scary, I didn't know what to do," Echo closed her eyes tightly against the memory for a moment.

"Oh my goodness, sweetie, I'm so sorry that happened to you," Missy whispered. "Where did he take you?" she asked, horrified.

"He drove to his aunt's house and parked in the back, where no one could see us from the street. When he stopped the car, I opened the door and tried to run, but the heel of one of my sandals caught on a root and I fell. Ian grabbed me from behind, twisting my arms behind my back so that I couldn't get away, and when I screamed, he clamped his hand over my mouth and nose so that I could hardly breathe," Echo paused to gather her wits about her. She'd obviously been severely traumatized.

"There was an open door that led to the basement, and he dragged me down the stairs into this dark, smelly place, and made me sit in a chair. He tied my legs to the chair legs, tied my hands behind me and put a nasty rag in my mouth so that I couldn't scream. It was awful, Missy, I thought I was going to die and no one would ever find me. Ian paced around like a mad man, ranting about how he was finally going to have the life he wanted. He talked about…" a small sob escaped her, and she had to take a few deep breaths before continuing. Missy reached for her hand, and Echo clung to her friend like a lifeline.

She recovered enough to continue, tears streaming down her face. "He bragged about killing his aunt, and said that now he owned everything he wanted, a house, some land, and a good woman. He talked about buying a boat and sailing around the world and told me that if I didn't behave myself, he'd throw me to the sharks."

"Oh my goodness, Echo, that must have been terrifying for you," Missy said sadly, as her friend sipped her tea, trying to recover.

"Well, thankfully, right after that, I heard sirens and a loudspeaker and in a matter of minutes, the police had surrounded the house and were blocking the basement door so that Ian couldn't escape. He got really angry when he figured out that he was trapped, so he tipped my chair over and I hit my head really hard. I couldn't really see what happened after that, but the next thing I knew, this really nice detective, Gilbert Johnson, was untying me and helping me outside. I saw Ian in handcuffs being stuffed into the back of a patrol car, and I was so relieved that I nearly fainted."

"I can't even imagine how awful that must've been for you," Missy shook her head. "Do you want to stay here for a while? I could make us some dinner and we could watch a movie or something," she offered.

"Thanks for asking, but what I really want to do, now that I know I'm safe, is go home and take a nice long bath, have a glass of wine and sleep for as long as possible."

"I totally understand, but if you need anything at all, or even if you just have a nightmare and want someone to talk to, you call me, okay?" Missy insisted with love.

Echo nodded. "I will. Thank you for being my friend, Missy, I don't know what I'd do without you."

"Anytime," she replied, embracing her friend.

"Can I get this Mango Madness to go?" she gestured to her uneaten cupcake.

"You know it!" Missy picked up the cupcake and headed to the kitchen for a baggie to put it in. She handed Echo the cupcake and walked her to the door, confident now that everything would be okay.

**

The walls were up in the newly built Missy's Frosted Love Cupcakes, the appliances were being installed in a week, and all that would be left to do was painting the whimsical lime green and pink colors of the interior, placing the furnishings in the seating area and stocking the kitchen. Construction had been completed well ahead of schedule, and it looked like

Missy would be up and running again just in time for her Ghoulishly Good Ghost cakes that were light, fluffy and tended to disappear. They were a favorite among the kids of LaChance, who came into the store for them specifically, every Fall.

"The progress looks great," Missy was pleased to hear the deep voice of Chas Beckett at her elbow. She turned, happily surprised and gave the handsome detective a big hug.

"I'm so excited, Chas," she exclaimed. "I'll be able to have it up and running again before the holiday season starts."

"That's great news," he smiled at her excitement. "What are your thoughts about maybe taking a vacation sometime in the near future?"

"Well, now that you mention it, I'm long overdue for a vacation. My trip to Vegas for the cupcake competition was supposed to be a bit of a vacation, but that didn't work out too well," she grimaced, remembering. "Why do you ask, trying to get rid of me for a while?" she teased.

"Hardly," he responded, brushing a kiss across her brow. "I just know how hard you've been working and the...unusual set of circumstances that you've had to deal with, and figured that it might be about time for a break. You could relax, unwind, have some personal time for a change."

"That does sound lovely," she admitted. "It'll just depend upon whether or not I can get enough new people hired and have them trained well enough to feel comfortable entrusting my shops to their tender care."

"How's Echo doing these days?" he asked, changing the subject.

"Much, much better," Missy grinned, thinking of her friend. "She's so much more relaxed and carefree. Now that her secret is out, she doesn't have to be careful about what she says and how she behaves, she can just be herself."

"That's good to hear," Chas nodded. "Personally, I'm glad that the whole mess is over so that we can go back to being ourselves. I could stand right here in the middle of the sidewalk and kiss you if I wanted to."

"Do you?" Missy asked playfully.

"Do I what?" he teased back.

"Want to," she looked up at him with a gleam in her eye.

"What do you think?" he asked, inclining his head toward her.

Missy smiled against his mouth, kissing him back and was glad from her head to her toes that life had returned to normal. She was more than ready to explore a relationship with this amazing man and move forward into a new chapter of her life, but first, she might just take that much-needed vacation.

**

Detective Chas Beckett strode into his office, a smile playing about the corners of his mouth after a nice lunch with Missy and an even nicer kiss to send him on his way. There was something about her sweetness that made him forget all about the daily rigor of investigating usually petty crime in the easygoing town of LaChance, Louisiana. He was very much looking forward to hatching a plan to take her away for a while, allowing her to find the rest and relaxation that she needed, under the warm Caribbean sun. The thought made him smile, and carried him through the rest of his mundane day. His life had certainly changed since he met the feisty, warm-hearted petite blonde who had captured his interest, and he couldn't wait to see where the path led from here.

AUTHOR'S NOTE

Writing a series was quite a learning experience for me. I'd never done it before, and I found out that it was way more difficult than I had thought it would be. Each book had to be a story that was complete in itself, in case a reader randomly selected a book out of order, but it also had to be cohesive with the rest of the series. One of the most challenging tasks was trying to give enough background information in each book to help a new reader understand the characters, settings, situations, etc...without providing so much information that the readers who started at the beginning would be bored. Missy and Chas and the gang were all so real to me that I felt like I knew them, yet I had to introduce them anew in each subsequent book, so I looked at it as though I was merely at a party, introducing them to my friends, and hoped that the warmth and appreciation that I felt toward them shined through.

The mechanics of regularly publishing books was something that I had never thought about. I was accustomed to working with deadlines, and always managed to meet or beat them, but I never really understood the importance of them and why they actually existed. As I found out from my publisher, there were people who were unable to do their jobs until I did mine. The cover designer couldn't produce the cover until I had written a blurb – which was another thing I'd never done before – and didn't know what cover art to use until I described the cupcake. There were decisions to be made, and rules to follow, that I'd never considered before.

I had gotten into a groove by the fourth book, at least from a writing habit standpoint. While the pace was challenging, I wrote a book each week. The way that I scheduled my time was to write for a solid three days, then turn in the book and take the rest of the week off. While that meant that I still sometimes missed out on social events because I was working a deadline, it usually made it possible for me to both write and have a life. If I knew that I had something coming up that I wanted to do, I could shuffle things around a bit. I usually wrote Sunday through Tuesday, or sometimes Wednesday morning, if the book was a bit longer, so I'd have the weekend free, but if I wanted to go to something in the early part of the week, I'd just push the schedule out another day. My deadlines were on Friday, and the book was always published the following Tuesday. Readers knew when to expect it, and, just like watching a favorite TV show, they knew when the next episode would be available.

At this point, I was still working very hard to not be hurt or dismayed by the occasional bad review, and I was getting better at it, but still panicked every time I saw anything under three stars. My publisher, with great wisdom, counseled me to stop looking at the reviews, assuring me that if there was anything constructive that I needed to know, she would tell me. Of course I didn't listen, and ultimately, I'm glad

I didn't. The more negative reviews that I read, the better I got at being able to discern which ones were important and should be taken into consideration, and which ones were just either a personal preference or a troll.

I was such a newbie to the writing world, that I had no idea what a troll was, or that they existed. I just figured that, either someone likes a book or not, and had no clue that sometimes folks were even hired to give bad reviews. My innocence as far as the world of professional writing was starting to crack a bit, but I was determined to not let a bit of disillusionment affect my writing. A good piece of advice that I was given at the time was that I shouldn't change the way I do things just because of one negative review. If there was consistent feedback about an issue, I should think about how to address it, but one comment shouldn't be enough to alter my writing, unless it was from a trusted source. Live and learn.

Despite the fact that my eyes were being opened about the reality of business, I was still so happy to be writing for a living and looked forward every week to my book being on the top of the Cozy charts. It was, and still is, so surreal when that happens. Every day, I'm so thankful that I get to write for a living. They say that if you love what you do, you'll never work a day in your life, because it doesn't feel like work. While I do consume a ton of time and energy with my writing, it doesn't feel like a chore. I'm doing what I love and I'm profoundly grateful that I can.

Writing is my passion, my love, and from a mad stroke of luck, my occupation. Doing this makes me happy, and what I love more than anything is sharing that happiness with my readers, because I couldn't do what I do, without you. Thank you, dear readers! I have committed to doing all that I can to make you happy with my writing for as long as I'm able, and I deeply appreciate all of you so much.

SPICED CARROT CUPCAKES

2 eggs at room temperature

2 Tbsp. unsalted butter at room temperature

1 cup brown sugar

¼ tsp. pure vanilla extract

½ cup cinnamon flavored applesauce

1 tsp. ground Vietnamese cinnamon

¼ tsp. ground allspice

2 ½ tsp. baking powder

½ tsp. baking soda

2 cups All-Purpose flour

2 cups shredded carrots

Cream together butter and brown sugar. Beat in eggs and applesauce. Sift together ground cinnamon, ground allspice, baking soda, baking powder, and flour. Mixing by hand, slowly add dry ingredients to the wet ingredients, stir until combined. Stir in vanilla and shredded carrots.

Preheat oven to 350 degrees. Pour batter to fill 2/3 of cupcake liner. Bake cupcakes for 15-17 minutes and check with a toothpick. If batter doesn't stick to the toothpick, then cupcakes are done. Makes 18-24 cupcakes.

GOOEY CREAM CHEESE FROSTING

8 oz. cream cheese

¼ cup unsalted butter at room temperature

2 cups powdered sugar

¼ cup heavy whipping cream

1 tsp. pure vanilla extract

18-24 pecan halves

Cream together cream cheese and butter. Slowly, alternating, add in powder sugar and heavy whipping cream. Mix in vanilla. Frost cupcakes when cool. Top each cupcake with a pecan half.

37426633R00093

Made in the USA
San Bernardino, CA
30 May 2019